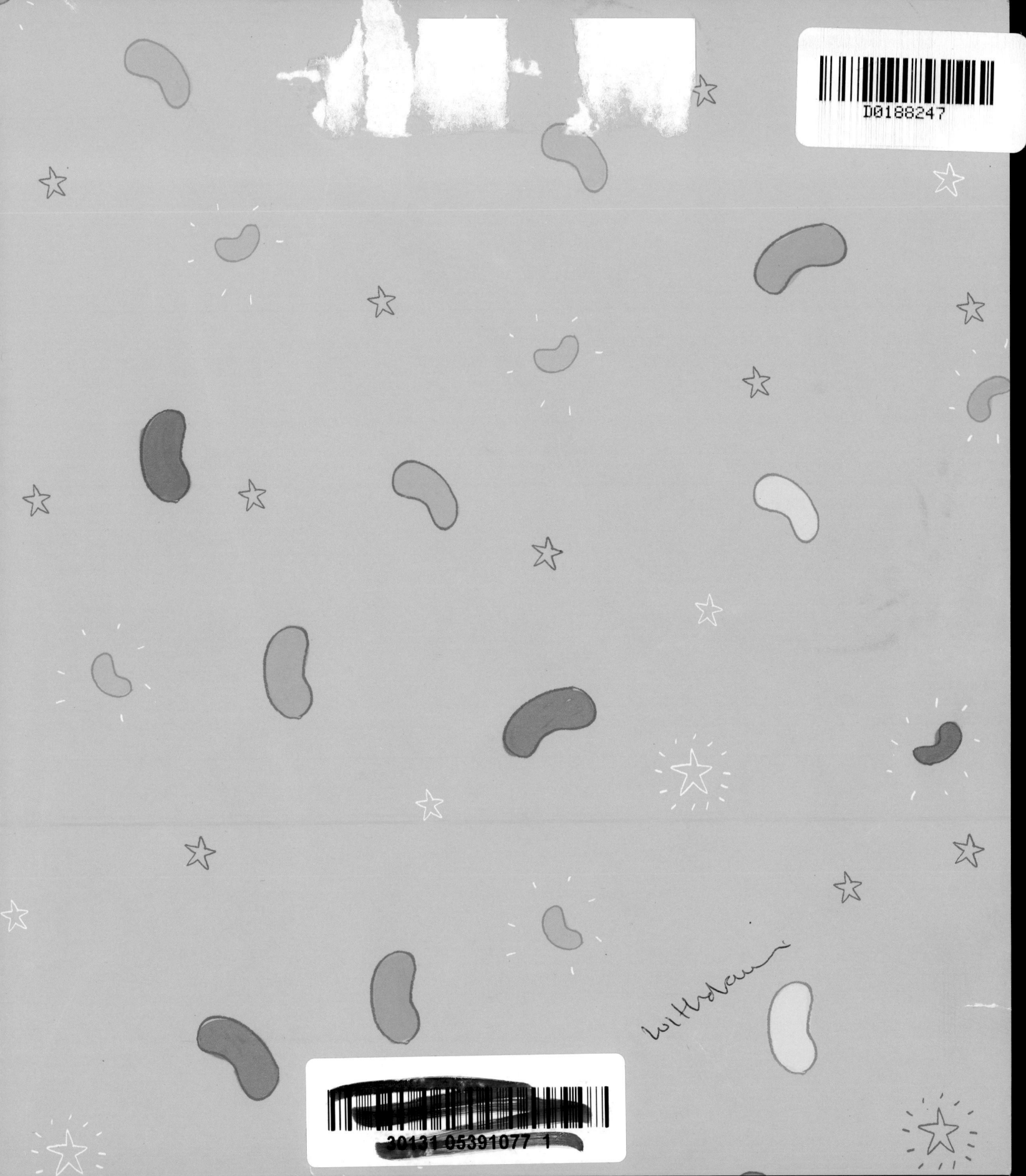

This incredibly good book belongs to:

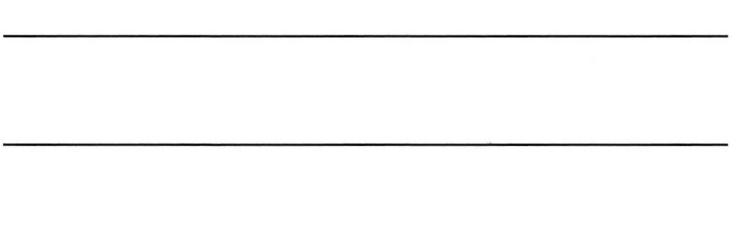

_____

_____

_____

For three little brothers who
outgrew their big sister – GC

For John, thank you – KC

©2013 North Parade Publishing Ltd.
North Parade,
Bath BA1 1LF. UK
Printed in China.
www.nppbooks.co.uk

JACK AND THE INCREDIBLY MEAN STALK

Written by Gemma Cary
Illustrated by Kelly Caswell

NorthParadePublishing

Once, there was a boy called Jack. He lived with his Mum in a tiny flat and he believed in magic.

One day, Jack sold their television in return for some magic beans. Jack's Mum was so angry that she tossed the beans out of the window. Before long, something below began to **rumble**...

"What is it?" said Mum.

"**An earthquake?**" suggested Jack.

Jack and his Mum ran outside just as a little green shoot burst from the earth.

The little shoot became a thin stem, and the thin stem became a chunky stalk.

A crowd began to gather nearby.

"**Fee,**" said the stalk.

"**Fi,**" it cried, growing taller still.

"**Fo, Fum!**" it yelled, so everyone could hear.

"I smell a boy and his **Stinky Mum!**"

Jack's Mum immediately scuttled home to take a bath.

"That was a bit unkind," said Jack to the beanstalk.

"Well," it replied, "I'm not any old beanstalk. I'm an incredibly **MEAN** stalk, and I plan to live up to my name. Do you know what else I can smell?"

"What?" asked Jack.

"Your whiffy feet!"

The crowd laughed and Jack blushed.

"Luckily for me," said the mean stalk, "I'll be growing higher and higher, far away from your festering toes!"

Jack felt miserable.

He sat with his Mum, looking at the space where their TV used to be. He was disappointed that his magic beans had created such a monster.

Meanwhile, the mean stalk grew up and up.

"Oh Jack..." it teased.

"It's **BEAUTIFUL** up here! What a shame I'm the only one tall enough to see it!"

"You could let me climb up," said Jack.

"**Never!**" replied the mean stalk, and it carried on growing.

One day, the stalk spotted a giant's castle nestling in the clouds.

"**Fee, fi, fo, fum!**" roared the mean stalk. "I detect 'parps' from a giant's bum!"

The castle's drawbridge creaked and lowered, and a giant appeared.

"Please don't be mean," he said bashfully. "It's ever so lonely up here and I'm entirely friendless. Might **you** be my friend?"

"**Never!**" replied the mean stalk,
and it carried on growing.

Parp!

"Wait!" said the giant. "Do you know **anyone** who might be willing to be my friend?"

"I know a pongy boy called Jack," said the stalk. "You two are probably smelly enough for one another!"

"Would you kindly allow me to climb down and meet him?" asked the giant.

"**Never!**" replied the mean stalk.

But the giant wasn't ready to give up. He wrote letters to Jack, and sent small presents floating down through the sky.

Jack read the giant's letters and received his thoughtful gifts. He wanted to thank him.

"Please, please can I climb up to meet the giant?" Jack begged.

"**Never!**" said the mean stalk. "Just look at how tall I am! I'm taller than a tower of giraffes... I'm taller than a whole rainforest... I'm taller than a stack of skyscrapers... I'm the tallest thing on the **PLANET!**"

..., the infall bean grew so tall that it soared through the Earth's atmosphere and burst into space.

"**Fee, fi, fo, fum!**" it cried. "Now I'll have some real fun!"

The mean stalk floated around, drifting between the stars and planets. After a few days of floating and drifting, the stalk realised how quiet it was. Suddenly, it felt very, very alone.

"what am I doing up here?" it thought, sadly.

The mean stalk wound its body down
and down, round and round, back to Earth.
It saw how happy everyone was.

"They haven't missed me at all,"
thought the mean stalk. "I'm useless.
Being mean is useless."

The mean stalk nudged its head through Jack's window.

"Jack," it said tearfully, "I want to stop being mean. But I don't know how..."

"I have a few ideas!" said Jack.

Weeeeeee!

So helpful!

"**wait a minute,**" said Jack. "We can't call you 'mean stalk' any more! You're kind and helpful and extremely useful. What shall we call you instead?"

"Hmm," said the **not-mean-at-all stalk,** thinking carefully. "I quite like the name Stanley."

"Very well," said Jack. "Thank you, Stanley."

So Jack and the giant, Stanley and everyone else lived together happily. And Stanley never called anyone stinky again.